Musings

Musings

Flight of Fancy and Romantic Interludes

J R PRINCE

ARPress
45 Dan Road Suite 5
Canton MA 02021

Hotline: 1(888) 821-0229
Fax: 1(508) 545-7580

Ordering Information:
Quantity sales. Special discounts are available on quantity purchases by corporations, associations, and others. For details, contact the publisher at the address above.

Printed in the United States of America.

ISBN-13:   Softcover   979-8-89356-841-7
                eBook   979-8-89356-842-4
                Hardcover   979-8-89356-843-1

Library of Congress Control Number: 2021909971

TABLE OF CONTENTS

CHAPTER I
FLIGHTS OF FANCY

CHAPTER II
MAGICAL DREAMS

CHAPTER III
ROMANTIC INTERLUDE

FOREWORD

J.R. Prince has written many short stories and poems throughout his career. He has found a passion for stories that step into new realms of possibilities and adventures. He enjoys creating stories that bring to life the magic and mystery of places most people only dream about. He also loves writing poetry and has done so for many years. In his poetry he is effective in creating emotion that enables his readers to feel and connect with his written words. He has composed so many works of art and has brought many of them together in this book for your enjoyment.

J.R. Prince's ability to create new worlds through vivid imagery and charming stories will capture any reader's attention who wishes to escape their reality and find a new adventure. The short stories written in this book are filled with magical creatures and new worlds that defy space and time. Along with mythical creatures, the stories entail plots of good versus evil, the battle the characters must endure, and the ability for them to overcome it all. After reading the short stories included in this book, I was definitely left wanting more. Deja Vu: Time Pilot, and The Chronicles of Sinoma for example, were both stories filled with mystery and suspense that kept my full attention until the very end. And both stories ended in ways that had me reeling for more. I must say though, out of all the short stories, my favorite definitely had to be Bard of Belarus. Not only was it filled with adventure and magic, it was filled with friendship and love. With so many exciting twists and turns in so little words, it is clear why these stories are a must read for any person seeking a new adventure. But these stories aren't just great because of the new realms of possibility they bring to life, they are written with wit and clear passion making them a fantastic read.

Not only has J.R. Prince been able to bring these wonderful short stories to life in his book, he has also beautifully written so many incredible poems. The poems within this book will enthrall anyone with their ability to make you feel the emotions and envision the story told by them. He has written poems on love, the longing for that love, the journey of life, the feeling of defeat, and so much more. J.R. Prince's ability to open your mind to so many emotions with just a turn of a page will leave any reader wanting more. You can tell by the way he has illustrated these poems with his words that the emotions expressed are ones he has poured onto the pages. It is so easy to connect to these poems because the experiences portrayed in them are ones we all live through. We have all loved, and most have also felt the pain of having to long for a love they cannot have or are far away from, making it so easy to understand the sentiment in these poems. He also captured the feelings you face inside yourself when you must deal with life, and the struggles we all come across. We don't all share the same struggles in life, but the beauty of these poems is that you don't have to know the struggle he was facing to know the emotion that came along with it. With so many amazing poems, it will be hard to put his book down and hard to not want to read them again and again.

The short stories and poems are so carefully constructed in this book, with their abundance of imagination, imagery, and passion, it is sure to grab any reader's attention and leave them wanting more. Any person who appreciates and loves poetry and adventure will surely love this book. Take the time to step into these stimulating stories and beautifully written poems, and I guarantee you will fall in love with them, just as I did.

Amber Drummond

CRAZYWOLF AND HAWK: AN AMERICAN FOLK TALE

by
James R. Prince

An old Indian legend says: Before the White Man came, a lone man and a wolf walked together. Nobody knew from whence they came or to where they went. Some say they were spirits, doomed to walk the Earth until a great magic was released. Still others believed they were The Great Spirit come to Earth in time of dire need. This is the story behind the legend.

One day, a brave band of young warriors were out to make their passage to manhood. On foot, without weapons or supplies, they were many miles from aid or shelter.

Unknown to the youths, they were being stalked. In times past, many groups of young warriors who took the rite of passage disappeared forever. They were believed to be the chosen of The Great Spirit. Sadly, this was found to be untrue. They had been tracked and slaughtered by a terrible tribe of cannibals who migrated yearly from the south.

As the weary band of youths prepared to bed down for the night, a strange sight appeared to them. A lone wolf howled from a nearby plateau. Silhouetted by moonlight, it could be seen it wasn't a normal wolf. Astride its back was the silhouette of a man--and as quickly as man and wolf appeared, they were gone. It was thought that surely the wolf must be crazy to let a mere man ride upon its back--and because they felt the spirit of the mighty hawk must rest upon the man to befriend a wolf--he was favored with their highest honor. This is how they came to be known as Crazywolf and Hawk. Awed and with many questions, the youths bedded down to a restless night of sleep.

As morning dawned, dark, ominous, and eerily quiet, they began to fear evil was afoot. They armed themselves with what they could find and ate a meal of tubers and berries washed down with water, then moved out with extreme caution for the last leg of their outgoing trek. As the day wore on and sunlight peeked through the clouds they began to relax their guard——even laughing at the silliness of their fears.

Just then the cannibals struck. They rose up from everywhere, seemingly birthed from the Earth Herself. Hopelessly outnumbered and surrounded, the youngsters took the fight to the cannibals.

With a warrior's cry the battle began.

Yet fight as brave young men would, the opposition was overwhelming——even indulging in sport with their prey.

As the realization dawned on the youths they were going to die a meaningless death––deprived of honor––they heard the howl of a great wolf.

Out of the grasses arose a wolf the size of a horse with an ax-weilding rider astride his back. Into the melee they charged, hewing down terrified cannibals. With a snap of his powerful jaws Crazywolf rent men in two. With a single blow from his mighty ax Hawk smote men to the ground.

Then, as quickly as it had begun, the battle was over. Not a cannibal survived. As the stunned youths tended their wounded, they turned to thank their saviors, but Crazywolf and Hawk were gone––leaving a small band of beleaguered yet awed youths to tell their fantastic tale.

Because of that day we will always remember, it's been said Crazywolf and Hawk watch over our children to this day.

That is the story my father told me and has been passed from generation to generation in our tribe.

CHAPTER I

Flights Of Fancy

A MOMENT OF DAYLIGHT

A moment of daylight;
An angling sun,
The day's heat dissipates.
A blue sky in sunset…
Colors rage and integrate.
Time to unwind-
Tensions drift away…
Reminiscence shattered!
Birds intrude.
Setting a new course
Adrift on tranquil seas…
Dusk closes in
Snatching the day's power:
Leaving me alone
Longing to share
A moment of daylight.

THE SOUNDS OF SILENCE

A butterfly oscillates
On currents of air.
A gentle breeze
Stirring lonely clouds.
Open fields
Of reeling grasses.
A golden dawn
Or fiery sunset.
A tender look
or a soft caress.
Many things
that touch a lover's heart.
Saying so much
with the sounds of silence.

OUTSIDE OF TIME

Alone in time
in a place outside of time.
Days without you
are centuries to my heart.
Walls become
murals of you:
Flowing hair
Shimmering eyes
My escape.
I sink into you
my happiness outside of time.
Reality stalks me cruelly,
telling me;
you are a vision of time-
powerful none-the-less.
Reality cannot steal
the peaceful memories you bring
in a place outside of time.

SOMEDAY

If sunshine were a gift
I'd warm your life with happiness.
If moonlight came in a package
I'd always have a romantic evening prepared for you.
If shooting stars could grant a wish
I'd wish away all your sorrows.
If I could capture a sunset
I'd frame you in its' beauty.
If I could grasp the starlit sky
I'd weave a halo of brilliance to light your darkest hours.
If I could:
I'd change the past
Wrap you safely in my arms
Make every day special just for you.
If I get the chance:
I'll prove how special you are to me
Fill your life with happiness
Say I do all over again
and love you forever.

ONE LAST MILE

Weary and forlorn
the miles
have taken their toll.
I face
the crags of despair
with bloodied hands
and crippled feet
I climb the precipice.
When all seems lost
I am spurred on
by the strength
of your love.
Inch by inch
I traverse the days
Seeking my goal…
that final mile.
One last mile…
I am home.

ELEMENTS OF RAGE

Walking a solitary trek
keeping your council
yet hard pressed on all sides.
Persecuted by those that can't understand
mistreated by them that are too stupid to care.
Fight the good fight
to draw the short straw.
Beaten, battered and broken
still the limelight
illuminates our path
shining through
the corruption of pain.
To reach the goal
we sacrifice all
in hopes…for one moment
everything is aligned
in peace and harmony.

PETALS

Her eyes…
blue wells:
Sunshine behind a smile
Fire with a frown
Soul searing – accompanied by tears,
floating slowly down
gentle rose petals
showering my heart
and salting my lips
I kiss them away.
With your sorrow
I am carried away…

SEABORNE

Alone…on a deserted stretch of sand
seagulls call my name
as the sandpiper alludes another wave
in its' search for a succulent meal
the sand fl ea dives for cover.
The wind roars…breakers roll
the seas' aphrodisiac
nips at my senses.
Seeking her strength
with all that I am.
Her thunderous waves
touch a primal instinct,
their power strum
the strings of my heart,
I become
a finely tuned instrument
playing the song of the sea
She draws me in
and caresses me
with her briny touch.

FARAWAY THOUGHTS

Faraway thoughts
cover the miles.
Reaching out
to a lady.
Beauty filled with grace…
when she smiles
my world lights up.
Her heart-
One with mine!
Her tears
scorch my cheeks
and salt my lips.
her love
wraps me in joy
fulfilling my life.

PHANTOMS

I'm alone
but you're always near.
The sweet scent
of your essence
or freshly washed hair
permeates my world.
A silhouette
or shadow
seen from the corner of my eye
that can only be you.
Your gentle breath
upon my neck
as I discern
my whispered name.
A tender caress
with a feathery case
are the phantoms
that break my heart
and salt my checks with sorrow.

SILENT MESSENGER

A silent messenger
in a crowded realm.
Doom is screamed
at the top of my lungs.
Whispered on currents of time.
Love is siphoned out,
drawn from my polluted heart
like poison from a festering wound,
eroding all sense of hope.
Putrid black tears are shed…
death slithers down my cheeks
my soul wilts away
leaving the lasting essence of decay.
I am an empty shell
bereft of all that is life,
no reflection or shadow
to betray my passing.
A silent messenger
In a crowded realm.

A POET'S SANCTUM

An inner sanctum,
perspectives change,
a glimpse through
a child's eyes.

A world
seen through the kaleidoscope of time.
Feelings felt
without filters of age,
opening the doors…of the mind,
though locked in time,
open to a poet's inner sanctum.

PHOTOGRAPH

The look in your eyes…
a fiery smile
glowing skin
flawless beauty
came to life
as the shutter flashed.
The essence of you shown forth.
Drawing you
into the camera eye.
You are enshrined forever
perfect in the moment.

WILDFLOWER

A summertime collage…
Fields of green
Speckled with
a rainbow of color.
Few notice…
a Kaleidoscope
for a lover's eyes.
They await
the patient toil
of one who cares.
Within minutes
a gift
fit for a Princess.
Letting her know
how special she is
with a bouquet of wildflowers.

ICE CASTLES

Many see
a winter wasteland.
Few see
a winter wonderland.
They that see
are the gifted…
blessed lucky few.
From stark desolation
shades of death
gray, brown and ashen white
emerge…crystalline beauty.
Landscapes infused
multifaceted formations of ice.
Once illuminated
the eye is dazzled
the mind filled with wonder.

A DAY WITHOUT YOU.

A day without you
a conscious nightmare
from one horror scene to another.
An eternity in hell
time and suffering meld
days turn into night,
sleep…
no rest… no release.
Dreams of you
wrenching my heart
waking…
another day without you.

SILENT MESSENGERS

I whisper your name
a gentle zephyr
drifts your way.
I imprint my love
on the wings of a butterfly.
The essence of cherry blossoms
permeates your world.
Summer wildflowers
bloom in your presence
autumn leaves frolic
as you pass
your aura glows
pure white
on a snowy day.
Seasons and elements
are my silent messengers
reminding you of me.

HAUNTING

The phantom of your essence
plagues my existence
haunting my waking hours.
All my thoughts
are haunted by you.
My days
filled with fantasies
daydreams of you.
As night draws nigh
the last thing I remember
as I sink into dream's embrace
hours in my subconscious
wrapped around you.
Everything I say…do… think
is haunted by you.

THE TRAVELER I
TROUBADOUR

The traveler
a troubadour of life.
Walking the mean streets
storing sights and sounds…
gifts of knowledge
passed onto
the innocent and naïve.
Opening eyes
blinded by fears,
darkness
has no dominion
in the illuminating revelation
of the Troubadour's life.

THE TRAVELER II
WEARY

27

A weary traveler
down-trodden but confident.
Bested and vanquished…
coming out on top.
Pain and sorrow
enduring existence' road.
His God scrutinizes
many twists and turns,
faith's smelter
refines to gold.
To some
a knight in iridescent armor,
another sees
just a weary traveler.

THE TRAVELER III

CHAOS

Puffs of gray
stained
raging colors of red.
Pale green
deepens to blue.
Dawn's explosive entrance
heralds a new day.
Life – energy stirs
waking the traveler.
His slumber of peace
corrupted –
chaos…is a new day.

THE TRAVELER IV

DARKNESS AND SORROW

29

The traveler awakens
sleep fades –
Darkness and sorrow
fill the void.
Emotions of character
racing at the speed of light,
sent forth as messengers
from his heart…
going separate ways –
vanishing into the void.
Devoured by darkness and sorrow
leaving time and space
they are depthless conclusions.
Beginning and ending…
Within darkness and sorrow.

THE TRAVELER V
BIRD SONG

Alone in life
at one with nature.
Awakening…
the traveler is briefly touched.
A melody of sound
enlightens his senses –
cooings, chirps, whistles and stutters
greet each new day.
The sun
peeks into night's sky,
the chorus rises
a crescendo!
sound slowly fades…
Dawn brightens the firmament
leaving morning
devoid of sound
A lonely traveler
continues a beleaguered journey.

THE TRAVELER VI
SURVIVOR

Alone – undivided I stand.
A soul bereft of serenity.
A traveler of uninhabited realms.
A lighthouse
in the maelstrom of life.
Shining forth
no one sees.
A paradox of reflection
I turn to see myself.
A signal fire
on a lone mountain.
I cogitate…
why none heed my warning.
A sentinel—refugee,
sole survivor
tossed about in the storm's fury.
Straining to reach
the outer wards
of sanity's realm.

THE TRAVELER VII

SHADOWS

33

Shadows of the mind
cluttering thoughts
stirring the heart
obscuring the travelers path,
as he wanders
within the realms of imagination.
A confusing destiny
cold gray halls
echo his passing.
Empty sounds of loneliness
seeking someone to hear.
Potent within his walls
he avoids all contact.

THE TRAVELER VIII
CRYSTALLINE FIRE

All that beauty –
deep and blue
refreshingly chill
on a hot summer's day.
To get there
a toll ins paid.
Passing through
the gauntlet
of crystalline fire.
Super-heated
by Sol's power.
Lying dormat
waiting for…
the unprepared traveler.
Scorching tender feet
he pirouettes, hops and skips
to her inviting coolness
Soothing his agony
As storming breakers
thunder past his legs.

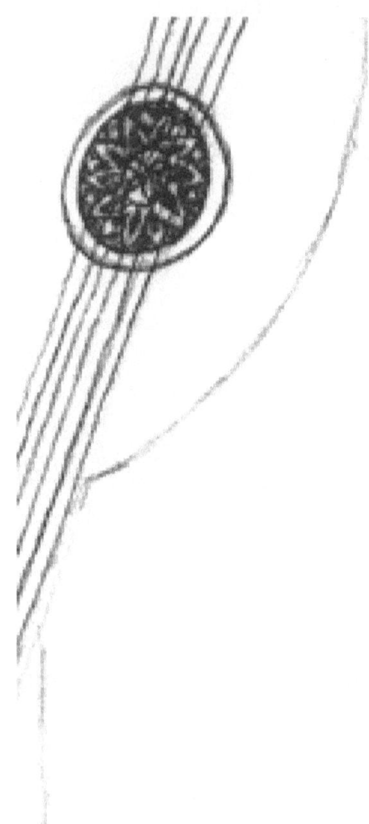

(FOREWORD) DRAGONS & GYPSIES

Throughout known history, dragons have loomed at the edge of our imagination. There is a reason for this—as shall be explained. Dragons remain nebulous in mankind's consciousness. Most are secretive and solitary. However, as with any intelligent creature, there are a few bad eggs in every batch.

Dragons have one characteristic flaw that permeates their species. Their greed for wealth, i.e. gold and jewels is unsurpassed. Though most prefer to amass their hoard of treasure surreptitiously, some, who we shall label evil, can overcome their solitary nature and openly seek tribute and followers to subjugate.

Most dragons live up to 15,000 years, so they only leave their hoard of treasure every 1,000 years or so to breed. In most cases, their bloodlines breed true and no evil offspring arise—though occasionally every generation or two, a bad egg hatches.

Dragons are not only solitary and secretive, but also proud creatures and try to weed out and destroy these aberrations. But as with every great society, an occasional evil one slips through and reaches maturation. The last to do so was a particularly evil dragon named, Succoth. If one of these creatures of magic and other worldliness succumbs to evil, nothing can subdue or destroy such dragons without the aid of powerful magic.

In the days before recorded history, humans lived in terror of these creatures. Their reign of evil would enslave entire continents before old age weakened them or ended their existence. In modern times, a group Of learned men have found ways to combat this evil. They discovered and made a pact with creatures out of phase with our reality called, The Faerie.[*]

---

[*] It is this author's opinion that dragons are exiled Faerie creatures.

These men called Gypsies, are mankind's protectors. They gave The Faerie something they lacked in exchange for the powerful magic to counter the evil dragons' power and magic. One such magic was imbued into a ten-stringed rosewood lyre. Over the ages, this magic has taken on a life of its own. Lyre is the first and as far as history records, the only magical instrument to achieve sentience. Lyre, in league with the Gypsy ruler and each successive ruler, have traveled throughout the known world to hunt down and destroy these evil creatures. However, the aberrant creatures are now well aware of this and fear Lyre. So Much so that when detected, they will charge their subjugated hoards to destroy Lyre at any cost.

Our tale takes place in Eastern Europe, circa 1250 AD. It is a dark time for mankind. In the last 100 years of so the Gypsies, in their arrogance, have turned away from and disregarded the prophesies and council of Lyre. This error led to near and utter destruction of mankind's protectors, which leads us to the story of the failed Gypsy Prince Ya'acov and his search for humanity's champion . . . Sima.

THE RHAPSODY OF SIMA: BARD OF BELARUS

by

J. R. Prince

A long time ago, in the distant land of Belarus, a legend was born in the small hamlet of Minsk.

One hundred years to the day, hope came forth on a cold February night in the form of a wondrous girl-child, a light to pierce a century of winter and darkness that shrouded and subdued the majestic land.

No one suspected the little girl, Sima, was special, much less that her hand would end a reign of terror and darkness.

She grew as any normal child, a true delight to her parents, and all who came to know her. Then everything changed on her fourth birthing-day celebration. A traveler, a Gypsy selling wares and services just happened to be in Minsk. He told terrible stories of a legendary dragon with awesome power that had subjugated the realm to this endless winter. Of how people were being demanded as tribute to feed her army of living dead. But that was not the reason he was there. At the urging of Lyre, a magical instrument of the same name, the Gypsy went to Sima's fourth bithing-day celebration and presented her with the magnificent gift. A rosewood ten-stringed lyre. The moment Sima's hands held the instrument she knew it had been crafted for her alone. With much pleading and assurance from the traveling Gypsy, her parents permitted her to have the unusual gift. And so began the legend of Sima, Bard of Belarus.

As only a child can acknowledge an unseen friend, Sima accepted Lyre. What she didn't understand, Lyre quickly taught her and instructed her in the magic of a Bard's song.

Sima listened and learned and was taught to believe she would become a great weapon to break the dragon's hold on their land.

As she and Lyre grew closer others drifted away. They couldn't understand Sima's strange obsession and devotion to a crafted piece of wood, thinking her daft to claim it was her best friend. By the time of her sixteenth bithing-day, even her parents had shied away from their strange and wistful daughter.

None believed her tales of a brighter future. None would hear of a fiendish dragon to be vanquished. All believed her sorely touched. Though her music and songs were a wonder and inspired all who heard, none listened long enough to be liberated from the dragon's spell. Finally, at Lyre's behest, Sima packed her meager belongings and left all she'd ever known to trek into the blizzard's violent grip... and her destiny.

That first night could have been the death of her had it not been for the lone Gypsy traveler of years past who had secretly waited and watched at Lyre's instruction. He was waiting just north of town in his wagon and offered her a ride and shelter from the storm.

Sima's first instinct was caution. But Lyre assured her he was a friend and needed companion in the coming fight against Succoth the great worm. Even so, she accepted the ride and shelter reluctantly and in time, within the safety and warmth––a hot meal in her hands–– Sima began a tirade of questions.

"Who are you?" she asked. "Where did you come from? How long have you been watching me? Why didn't you help me when others scorned me?"

"Slow down. One question at a time." said the traveler. Sima took a moment, then asked, "All right, who are you?" "My name is Ya'acov. I am the last Gypsy Prince."

"Are you really?" replied Sima, sarcastically. "And I'm a fairy princess."

"Believe what you will, but Lyre will confirm all I say," he snapped, silencing her. "I come from all over. As you can see, I travel with all I own. I've watched you ever since I gave you Lyre. I couldn't interfere unless your life was in danger because you had to be prepared when your time came to face your destiny.

"Where are we going?" asked Sima.

"As far as I can tell, north to destroy the great worm. Now, I have a question. May I see Lyre?"

With some trepidation, Sima handed Lyre to the stranger.

"My story is tied to Lyre," he said with a faraway look. "This instrument has been in the care of the Gypsy King for as long as we can remember. Some believe it's not only magical but also indestructible. Since I am the last of the line of Royal Gypsies it was mine to keep and render to its rightful owner." With a strum of strings and a few clumsy chords, Ya'acov continued his story and handed Lyre back to Sima.

"In my youth––or arrogance––I rallied many to the cause of destroying Succoth. I am a gifted singer and with the magic of Lyre I led many to believe in my crusade. As the last of a great line of Gypsy Royalty, many brave knights and heroes flocked to my banner–– daring an ill-fated campaign to Succoth's polar fortress. By the grace of Lyre I alone survived to know the folly of my ways.

"Lyre then showed me a vision of a child in the small hamlet of Minsk. I'd arrived just in time to present this child with the gift of Lyre on her fourth birthing-day celebration.

"Yes, I know who you are. You are Sima and you are destined for greatness. I know your life hasn't been easy and it will only become harder and more dangerous. If you will allow me, I'll accompany you on this perilous road to slay a dragon. Your songs are powerful indeed. Yet there may be times I can be of help."

"How can you know so much about my future?" interrupted Sima.

"To most I am a lone traveler. But as I've said, I am the last Royal Gypsy and by that, keeper of prophesy. Your life, Sima, is one of prophesy. Your destiny has been foreseen for generations.

"Why?" cried Sima. "I am an outcast amongst my own people." "That is your strength," replied Ya'acov. "And my weakness. I once tried to influence prophesy to suit my wishes and many suffered for my arrogance. So, now as you, I am an outcast also. If you'll allow me, I want to be your friend because I know you're not touched.

I know you're blessed with an awesome gift ... and cursed with a special secret."

With some apprehension, Sima accepted the Gypsy Prince at his word and warily traveled in his creaking wagon pulled by his old hairy yak.

After a few days of travel Sima and Ya'acov arrived at a small village. Supplies were depleted and in dire need. The traveler plied his trade, offering his services as a tinker. But there were no buyers of his wares or services.

After days of silence that had left Sima brooding——even a little frightened——Lyre urged her to go to the local alehouse and offer her services as a minstrel. Though reluctantly, Sima did as Lyre urged.

Upon arrival the owner, an obese, grim-looking matron, looked the young woman over and said, "It's your skin, sweetie."

Sima climbed onto the stage and with burning eyes from the acrid smoke and trembling fingers, began to play.

Most believed she cried as her song filled the air and were ready to laugh her off the stage. That all changed when her strumming fingers and lilting voice inspired visions of flowers, green trees, and streams teaming with life. Not a single patron uttered a word until the last chord was struck. Then the alehouse erupted in chaos.

Afraid, Sima looked for an escape, but the matron intercepted her flight and begged, "Play some more."

Breathless, Sima replied, "I'm here with a companion. We're traveling north and in desperate need of supplies and fodder for our yak."

Beaming a smile the matron said, "Play and the patrons will take care of the rest."

That night the entire village was treated to visions of sunlight, flowing fields and a hope that fear, darkness, and winter would soon end. With much pleading from the villagers and some urging from Ya'acov, Sima played the next day in the village square. A bonfire roared as snowflakes fell and all were delighted with visions of star-infused summer nights and harvest-laded storerooms nearly forgotten.

The dragon's spell was broken. Hope abounded.

The following morning, well supplied and with a village of new friends pleading for her to stay, Sima and Ya'acov left to continue their journey north, but not before promising someday soon they would return.

Meanwhile, Succoth felt the magic of Lyre and Sima's songs drawing near. She retreated to her ice fortress at the North Pole and prepared her defenses to destroy any who would dare oppose such a great creature as she.

Through villages, towns, hamlets, and cities, Sima and Ya'acov traveled. They left behind a trail of hope and broken hearts when she wouldn't stay. All who heard her songs wanted to possess her and make her their friend. In her wake Sima left a trail of open rebellion and scorn toward the monster Succoth and her minions who sought tribute.

Soon afterward, Sima learned why the Gypsy Prince had accompanied her. They were ambushed by undead minions of Succoth and before she had a chance to play Lyre they would have been overrun. But Ya'acov flashed into action. With twin vorpel swords she'd never seen, he repelled the first wave. Then Sima's song subdued the rest.

Struck with wonder, Sima inquired, "Are you a warrior?"

"No," he replied. "But in these dark times a lone traveler must know how to protect himself or those in his care."

Amused, Sima said, "So, I'm in your care?"

"No, you're my friend and the hope of my future," Ya'acov plainly answered.

With a small frown and teary eyes Sima said, "Thank you. I'm glad you're my one true friend. But you could have been hurt, or worse."

"I knew that when I offered to accompany you. You are the hope of a better future for everyone; and what is life worth without hope? I can't think of anything more worthy than risking my life at your side."

Through many hardships, dangers, battles, and suffering, the pair of heroes continued their journey to the dragon's lair. The final miles were the most arduous. Their hairy yak refused to go farther than the mountains that ringed the tundra surrounding Succoth's fortress. The oppressive pall of terror and hopelessness of the dragon's magic was distressing. The icy landscape——decorated with human remains—— patrolled by an army of undead——was fraught with dangerous traps and deadfalls. To make matters worse, Sima and Ya'acov were heavily laden with supplies which greatly slowed their progress.

Days later, after hiding and running, supplies depleted, they found the entrance to Succoth's fortress where they hid the last of their supplies, hopeful, of course, they'd return from their date with destiny.

Upon reaching the stronghold, Ya'acov said, "You know my skill with the swords can protect us from the undead creatures who have dogged our journey. But your magic—the enchantment of your voice—is the only thing that can destroy the dragon."

"What do you mean?" asked Sima.

"Lyre has taught you well. Your voice is a weapon against evil, strong enough to break the dragon's spell, as you have seen, but also powerful enough to actually vanquish her. Just believe in yourself and your song will do the rest. You are the most powerful Bard in history. I will do my all to safely get you to the throne room."

"Did you make it this far the first time? Or are all those bones we saw the thousands of knights who perished?"

Ya'acov chuckled. "No, my dear Sima. The drifting snows would have many years ago hidden their remains. Those are the tribute the undead feed upon. But yes, I stood face-to-face with the great worm Succoth, and by Lyre's power alone I managed to escape. Yet, where a thousand knights failed, we will succeed because Succoth's greatest weakness is her own arrogance. She knows we're here and will allow us to approach unmolested. So from here on we are going to be tethered to each other and hopefully make it through the pitch-black maze. Just remember, Sima; Lyre can protect you from her magic, and I'll protect you from her physical attacks as best I can until you destroy her. You must make certain; however, that you do <u>not</u> allow her to breathe on you or you will instantly be turned to ice."

After many days of blind wandering in the darkness, Sima and Ya'acov finally reached the great throne room of Succoth. Parched and weak from hunger, they staggered into the throne room's blinding light.

With a thundering voice, Succoth roared, "Kneel in my presence or be devoured!"

But the duo saw nothing nor could they locate the voice.

Again the voice thundered. "You <u>dare</u> defy me? I will freeze you and permit my minions to feast on your souls!"

Then just to their left, Succoth materialized out of the wall and nearly blasted Ya'acov and Sima with her icy breath. They came close to being severely frostbitten but managed to avoid the worst of it. With a warrior's cry Ya'acov raced forward and attacked with his vorpel swords.

Sima also acted swiftly as Lyre screamed in her head, "Now is the time!"

Sima's fingers began to play——her voice rising in strength as never before. At the height of her song, Succoth lashed out her tail and smote Ya'acov a deadly blow.

Sima's song and heart faltered then but Lyre's scream, "No!", focused her and with anger-filled sorrow her song roared through the throne room and struck Succoth in her icy heart, warming it with the sunshine of summer——melting it within her frozen breast. With one final bellow of hatred-filled pain Succoth collapsed in a mighty heap and died.

Sima raced to her fallen friend with breaking heart. She now knew what the loss of one loved felt like. She cradled Ya'acov's head, and for one brief instant his eyes opened.

A soul-searching look beckoned as he whispered, "Sing for me."

Grief-stricken——tears abounding——Sima sang as she had never sung before.

No Bard has ever had the power over life and death, yet something in Sima's song, or soul, surpassed all realms of reason. On that day her song cheated death and brought Ya'acov back from the grave, healed and whole. Perhaps that was her real power .. the depth and purity of her love.

Sima and Ya'acov returned to a land embraced by its first spring in over a century.

To this day there are seasons and even winters in Belarus. But with each cold winter comes the promise of summer and happiness just around the corner.

If not for my telling of this tale, none would know of Sima and Ya'acov's mighty deeds. I, Lyre, attest to the facts and truth of these events as I was a witness ... first hand.

CHAPTER II

Magical Dreams

POETICAL NECROMANCER I
MAGICAL GIFT

Born with the gift
    a chance to change the future
        I wield the power of cogitation like a wizard
            inscribing magical words.

Ingredients of ink form spells
    symbols that transform lives:
        Enchanting the shy
            captivating the bold
                enslaving the weak
                    mesmerizing the strong
                        carrying others away
                            to worlds unknown

Tapping thoughts only dreamed
Unleashing desires never imagined
Opening hearts
    To walk a lover's path.
        Snatching another
    From destruction's precipice
my role in life
    the Poetical Necromancer.

POETICAL NECROMANCER II
POETRY'S PRICE

Hunched over tools of power
    paying a terrible price.
Hoping to touch anyone in need.
Sleepless hours of conjuration
    ideas linger
        at the outer edge of phantasy
    no time for self…
Bloodshot eyes
    burning and sore
Crippled hands
    twisted fingers.
Giving my all
    a piece of self
        instilled into each enchantment.
Slowly drained
    behind the scene.
Recognition yearned
    yet never received.

POETICAL NECROMANCER III
POETRY'S PROMISE

51

Time alone
    the Necromancer conjures.
Wielding an instrument of power.
    new spells form.
Words—my inner being
    cast forth
        seeking a Karma to touch.
Lost in the weave
    many solutions …
        finally conforming
    a point of view.
A heart touched
    courage found
        tears transmuted to laughter
            I stand content
            time to unwind
        my work is done
        the ink dissipates

POETICAL NECROMANCER IV
AWAKENING

52

Transcending realms of thought
    power sources wane
        blink. from existence.
My mind implodes
    to burst forth
        a maelstorm of command.
An inner conduit forms.

Releasing the Necromancer
    into neural traces.

With the weapons of cogitation
    I weave my spells,
        no longer constrained
            by quill and parchment.
A cosmic transmutation
    of time and space
        seething outward
    power is wielded
infusing the void.
Though none are touched,
    Asylum is found.

POETICAL NECROMANCER V

MAGEWRATH

Rejected …
                    spells of power filled with wrath.
Assailed …
                    frenetically, I strike back.

Raging against
    an inkwell of blackness.
Enemies
    on all sides
        are the powers that be.
Shielded and aloof,
    smug with satisfaction,
        they crush another dream.
        A helpless unknown
    depleted of power,.
withering by the wayside.
A spark—Magwrath!
    The gauntlet is thrown down.
Fueled by resolution
    I fulminate against the ancients
        With their strictured ways.
Opening new anthologies.
    Recording the authority
of today's Poetical Necromancer.

POETICAL NECROMANCER VI

RESURRECTION

A dark empire
    standing upon
        ancient tomes
            of null power.
Blotting out today's Necromancer.
        Oppression is meted
           with heavy-handed blows
              to crush the psyche.
Power and wealth
    fuel their infinite madness.
        The empire devours
    all who oppose their way.
As the smoke and stench dissipates
    nothing is left but charred minds,
        the forces of Chaos roll toward antiquity.
This is justice for all:
        Alone
    stands the Necromancer,
flinging spells into darkness
    they sunder the tomes of null power.
Blazing a trail
    the faithful follow
        into uncharted territories.
    Opening hearts and minds,
        the oppressed minions
    are no longer
a footstool for the Empire.

Night has ended;
    a new age is born!
The Necromancer's work begins.
Resurrecting poetry
    from the ashes of antiquity.

55

POETICAL NECROMANCER VII

IMAGERY

I paint pictures
with words of power
on the canvas of your mind.
A slideshow collage
provoking thoughts and emotions
of my choosing.
Forever bending your will
I capture your intellect
and conform it;
a new regiment of understanding.
The spell of imagery
liberates your mind
from the brainwash
of society's propaganda.

POETICAL NECROMANCER VIII

PSYCHIC WARS

Darkness reigns absolute…
    minions of hell
    seduce our very thoughts.
The Necromancer stands alone
A veteran of many Psychic Wars.
        Trapped, overwrought and exhausted.
        Sleep is not option.
            The intellect devoured
                lurks on the other side of consciousness
                seeking to rend my mind
                    with one decisive blow.
                    I stand and fight
                        the twisted forces of Darkness
                    with spells of power.
Truth and honesty shield me
deflecting Evil at every turn.
        Love and friendship are my weapons.
        They vanquish Darkness
        to the fiery depths of Sheol.
Victory, or just a brief reprieve?
            Torn and battered
        my strength fades.
    I lay down to rest.
The weary soul
    of a
Poetical Necromancer.

POETICAL NECROMANCER IX
POWER OF POETRY

A solitary traveler
of ancient realms
passages of imagination
endless plains
uncharted and open
in the quest for perfection.

Time and space are distant theories
to be shaped and twisted
by the master's hand.
Words and concepts flow
as my ink transmutates
to spell of power.

Drawing the casual observer

Molding their point of view

The
POWER
of
POETRY

enlightens them with
multifaceted realms of imagery.
Captivated with passion   bred from a heart of truth
a transfusion of feeling flows
from the open veins of POWER in the Necromancer's soul.

POETICAL NECROMANCER X

LIMELIGHT

My mastery wanes
    cataclysmic forces surround.
        There is no retreat…
          … Spells of power fade…
            … ink evaporates—parchment crumbles…
Masters of a darker age
    waylay words of supremacy
        before they are completed.
Hope is taken,
    stolen by cruel circumstances,
        leaving the Necromancer to stand alone.
I cannot thwart their usurpation.
    Standing on the horizon
        a beacon of inspiration
          hope is restored
            darkness will be vanquished
        in another name.
    A mystical warrior
in the struggle for truth
The Necromancer bequeathes
    the secrets of his birthright
        and fades from the limelight.

SHADOWS WITHOUT LIGHT

Shadows without light
they hide in plain sight,
seen from the corner of your eye
terror in the night.
Eyes that have no faces
always watching… ever waiting
for that moment of weakness.
Silent screams rend the night
as ethereal fangs
fl ay our souls,
we die by degrees
our spirit bleeds away.
Resistance fades
our life force
is extinguished
becoming… shadows without light.

SHE'S ROCK AND ROLL

She's an axe grinder
an on-stage vixen.
Her siren song chimes
a mesmerizing force.
She plays upon my heart strings
a tune of yearning
filled with love.
She has struck a chord
that resonates
through my soul,
captivating my mind
she's only rock and roll.

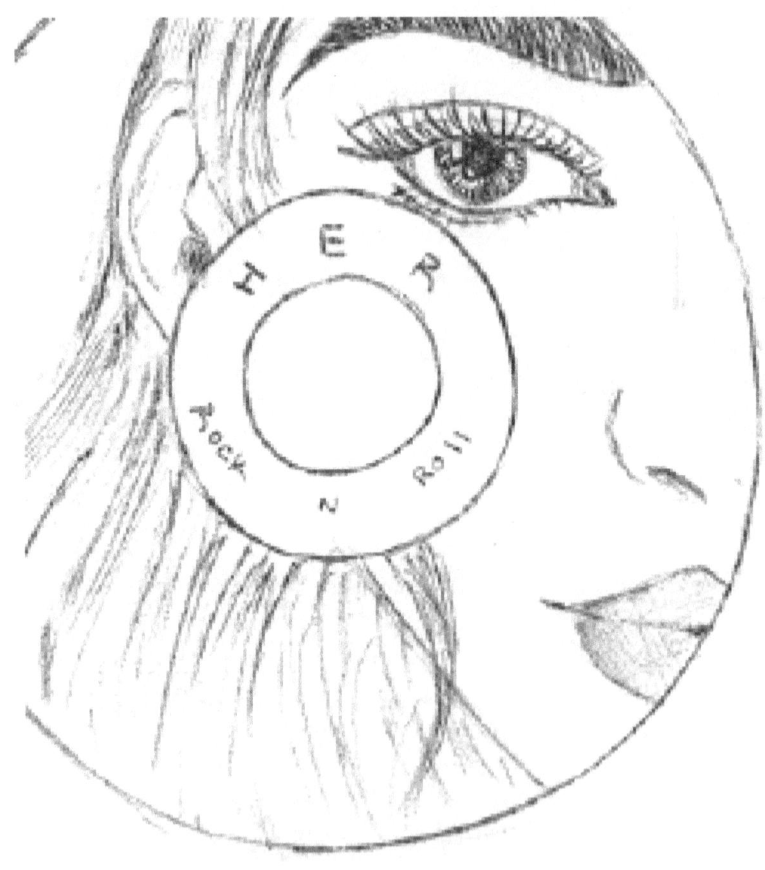
H
E
R
Rock
n
Roll

MUSICAL SORCERESS I

HER SECRET

65

She is beautiful, vibrant and free
a practitioner of an ancient art:
Legendary hero from antiquity
Life-force of magic and illusion
Sorceress of unlimited power
Master with an axe in hands.
The secret of her music…
her fingers are the instruments
that dance across the strings
weaving magical sequences
vibrations that alter time and space.
Images are formed – sounds burst forth
to captivate and dazzle
those favored few
with the legacy of her music.

MUSICAL SORCERESS II
SIREN SONG

A lost and old sea tar
without charts or bearing… hopeless
tossed about in life's storms.
A distant voice… her siren song
a melody that captured my heart
awakening dreams and desires
that lay dormant through the years.
Bringing happiness that dried my tears
and rejuvenated my soul
with her power
my Musical Sorceress.

MUSICAL SORCERESS III
BODY SONG

She sings to me with open arms
inviting me to sample her charms.
Beautiful full red lips
and sensual seductive hips.
Her perky breasts
a perfect place for my head to rest.
Her long legs and sexy butt
they make me dream to see her strut.
The song of her body sings to me
it captivates me then sets me free.

ANATHEMA

Forsaken and alone
hunger pains drive me.
All my desires deprived,
hopes have become
absolute despair.
I wander within
a landscape of decaying dreams.
A veteran
of many psychic wars.
Stripped naked
shattered emotionally
my greatest weapons
turned upon me.
Faith and love… my anathema.
They sere my soul
And pierce my eyes.
Leaving
the cloying fragrance of corruption
to permeate
my dying lucidity.

RATIONALE

Longing… that can never be fulfilled
the past… dead and buried.
Like a zombie I wander through
the corridors of my intellect.
Hopes and dreams… better days to comes
he gnaws away their flesh
in his vicious cycle of decay
that repeats itself in my dreams
that twist time and space.
Visions of the past, present and future
seen through a kaleidoscope of hope and misery
that wrench my emotions
as I climb toward wakefulness
leaving me mystified and drained of substance
my psyche plays Russian roulette
with my neutral traces.
I am just another pedestrian
on the broken ferris-wheel of insanity.
Leaving my walking rationale
trapped in the spin cycle of life.

ABYSS OF LIES

My pen… an instrument of battle
on every line I inscribe
the paradigm long forgotten.
I seek mythical concepts
truth, justice and mercy.
Can they rise
like a Phoenix
from the ashes
a defeated revolution?
Will they be devoured
by the abyss of lies
that sinks the hopes
of all who dare
just like you and me.

LONELY TEARDROPS

Lonely teardrops…
are they manifestations of my fears?
the slow desiccation of my soul?
am I being eaten alive – inside out?
do I hope or do I fear?
are the liberators here?
an executioner and court jester?
A kaleidoscope of images flood my mind
seizing me with emotional turmoil.
The pain is real
as the fire that burns through my veins,
this is the disease
that sere my soul
with lonely teardrops
my only true companions.

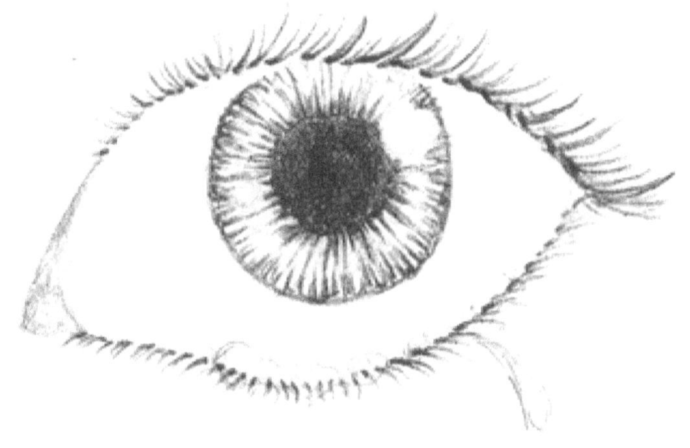

SHADOWS

Shadows…
our companions
or darker reflections
of our souls?
Always close
betraying our every move.
They dance
as we pull the strings.
A modern day mimic
chained to us by light.
Hidden in the dark
they lurk
just over our shoulder.
Waiting to pounce
at the first sign of light
infused with power
yet again.

A SILENT MESSENGER

A silent messenger
in crowded realm.
Doom is screamed
at the top of my lungs
whispered on currents of time.
Love siphoned out
drawn from my polluted heart
like poison
from festering wound
eroding all sense of hope.
Putrid black tears are shed
death slithers down my cheeks
as my soul wilts away
leaving the lasting essence
of decay.
I am an empty shell
bereft of all
that is life.
No reflection… shadow
to betray my passing
a silent messenger
in a crowded realm.

ELEMENTS OF RAGE

Walking a solitary trek
keeping your counsel
yet hard pressed on all sides.
Persecuted by those that can't understand
mistreated by them that are too stupid care.
Fight the good fight
to draw the short straw.
Beaten, battered and broken
still the limelight
illuminates our path
shining through
the corruption of pain.
To reach the goal
we sacrifice all
in hopes… for one moment
everything is aligned
in peace and harmony.

A FORGOTTEN RELIC –
THE TRAVELER

Darkness and sorrow… fill my days,
a traveler… with no place to go.
Trapped, betrayed… chained to the spot
I slowly wither away.
A pawn in prophecy
I rail against the machine
futile ravings are absorbed
by wall or foreboding
the machine feeds on misery
grinding bones to dust
scattering hope to the four winds
smashing it against the pillars of earth.
Pillars of strength crumble in time
a grim prospect for the future,
a forgotten relic to be discovered
restored and displayed in a corner…
the museum of darkness,
another conquered soul
to be mocked and scorned.

BORN AGAIN – THE TRAVELER

Sunrise… sunset life
continues
at a stately pace.
An optical illusion
my horizon
a step closer every day.
I hasten my pace
with no apparent gain.
Horizon sought
may never be attained
is victory in itself.
A mental cripple
rediscovers dreams,
walls crumble
and the traveler is born again.

NIGHTMARE

A nightmare landscape
of shattered time and space.
Dimensions overlap
releasing the darkness
from long awaited dormancy.
Chaos unleashed
to drink our souls
then enslave us
with its evil intent.
Dragging us down
in the abyss
we rot and decay,
our corruption…
complete the beast cackles
as we suffer
hoping… we never escape
his eternal torment.

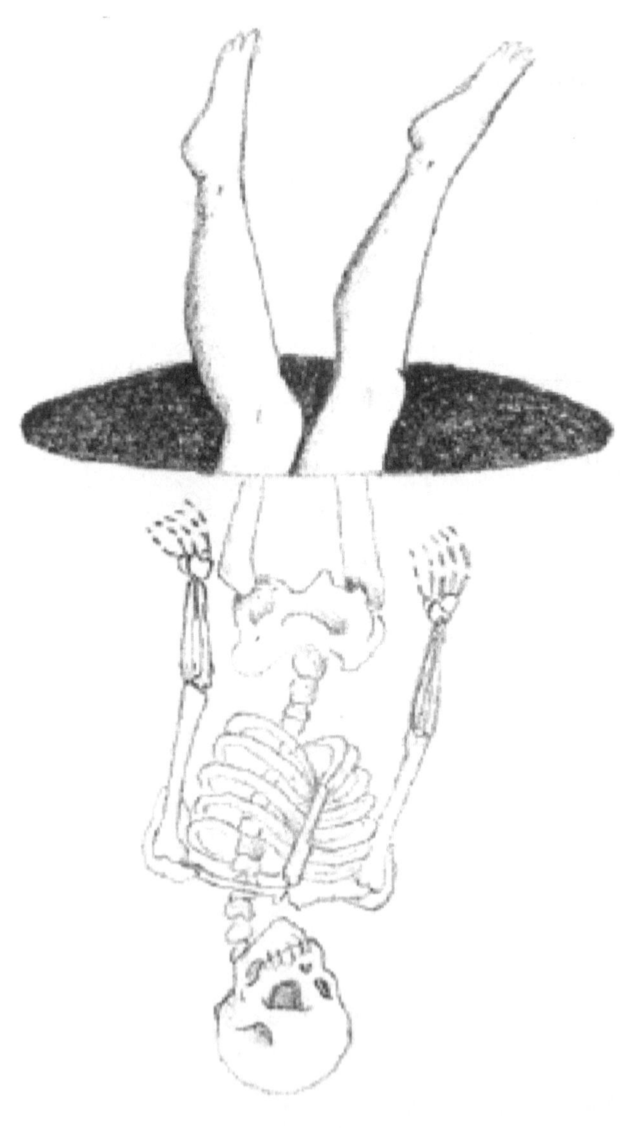

CAGED AND CONFINED

A caged tiger
pacing my confines.
Seeking a way
to be closer to you.
I yearn for your presence
using all the tools
at my disposal
my mind bends thought
stretches the limits
of reality
looking through
the camera eye
of time.
My heart breaks
with each failed attempt.
Leaving a desperate existence
of lonely haunted eyes.
a desolate spirit.

SHATTERED DREAMS

A day dawns another waking nightmare
in an uncertain future without you.
Alone with my constant companion
a shattered heart of pain.
Emotiona*l* turmoil seethes within my bowels
self-recriminations are my constant reminder
of a world where yesterday I betrayed myself
breaking the bond that was set in stone before time
a broken, chastised lost soul
with desperate pleas I seek your attention
I grovel for scraps of your forgotten affection
my downcast eyes burn with shame
tears of sorrow stream from my repentant heart
leaving me a contrite humbled man
that knows the depth of his loss.

CHAPTER III

Romantic Interlude

A ROMANTIC INTERLUDE

I will gaze into the blue depths of your eyes
as an astronomer seeking that one special point of light
I will run my fingers through your dark tresses
as a merchant testing the quality of the finest silks.
I will sample the taste of your lips and mouth
as a wine connoisseur sampling the finest French vintages.
I will suck each breast and nipple
like parched thirsting man sucking moisture from a damp store
I will caress and kiss the glowing moonlike globes of your butt
as the rising sun caresses and kisses the morning dew.
My tongue will taste and explore the depths of your womanhood
like a bee searching for nectar in the folds of a flower.
I will wrap your long sensuous legs around my waist
as a rider cinches the saddle of a wild pony.
Then slowly enter your womanhood to plumb your depths
revealing in the fiery embrace like the hot grasp of flowing lava
awakening your desires to hear your cries of passion
as the gail force winds in a passing typhoon
afterwards listening to the purr of your contented sighs
like a cool zephyr that soothes my sweaty brow on a summer day.
Laying arm in arm basking in the warm afterglow of love fulfilled
like the candlelit ambiance of a romantic interlude.

INTIMATE KISS

I take you in my arms
taste your lips
the softness of your breasts
hardened nipples.
Your flowing juices are honey and nectar
sweet delights
to anoint my senses.
The scent of your body perfume to my nose.
The fragrance of your sexan
aphrodisiac intensifying my desire.
As a starving man
I seek to sate my appetite with an intimate kiss…
delving the steamy depth
of you sex
I hunger for your release.
As you moan in pleasure

EXPERIENCE

I want to experience you...
feel your emotions
sense your desires
breathe your passion
I want to slip into
the fabric of your being...
meld my mind with yours
experience your thoughts.
I want to become...
one with you
see life through your eyes
hear the whispering wind
with your ears
taste your dreams
and experience your love.

A ROMANTIC INTERLUDE II

As my eyes drink in your beauty
Your beauty couldn't be more stunning
If you were made of gold.
My gaze lingers upon your body
As my eyes memorize your wonders
The intensity of my gaze
Causes your nipples to harden
As if from the cold.
The power of my desire filled gaze
Parts your long, gorgeous legs
As my sight delves within each succulent fold.
My hands begin their journey of adoration
Tracing every intimate curve of your body
And leaving a trail of fire in their wake.
Each caress takes you higher
With each touch you catch you breath
Anticipating when your desire I will slake.
With special caresses I pay homage
to the beauty of your perfect breasts and butt
and gently your womanhood they take.
With rising passion my lips trace your curves
And taste the sweetness of your flesh
Attempting to quench your fire.
Each lingering kiss is a testament of love
Telling you how much I care
And a gift to take your higher.
My kisses become more urgent
And proceed to that special place
Seeking to fulfill your ultimate desire.
With a soul searching kiss my tongue

Parts the inner depths of your womanhood
Like a dam breached your juices begin to flow.
With patience born of love
I continue my ministrations
Seeking to make your sexual volcano erupt…
With determined haste
I take you to ecstasies summit
As you bathe my tongue with your fiery flow.
Afterwards I hold you
In a sweet embrace
Basking in your breathless glow

A ROMANTIC INTERLUDE III

Our naked bodies become one
our sex is merged
as I slowly plumb
your scalding depths
your legs embrace my hips
encouraging my every thrust.
The earnestness of our passions
drive our bodies to exertion.
As muscles flex
our souls strain towards ecstasy
the sweat of your passion
pools between breasts.
As our bodies meld in motion
my tongue explores your heightened nerves
leaving a trail of fire…
each tantalizing kiss
across your throat
down to your breasts.
I slake my thirst
on your salty offerings
as I lick the sweat
from between your breasts,
with every once of amour
my desires erupt forth
to match and fill
your scalding embrace

MY DREAM GIRL

The day I say I do
It'll be to a girl like you
My dream girl.
She is the one who completes me
And sets my heart free
My dream girl.
She knows the true me
And has seen all there is to see
My dream girl.
Though most would flee in fear
She still wants to be near
My dream girl
She is beauty and grace
And her smile makes my heart race
My dream girl.
She is witty, smart and fun
The prettiest girl under the sun
My dream girl.
Now that she and I have met our future is a sure bet
My dream girl.
For her, I will always be there that is how much I care
My dream girl

PETALS

Her eyes…
Blue wells:
Sunshine behind a smile,
Fire with a frown
Soul searing – accompanied by tears;
Floating slowly down
Gentle rose petals
And salting my lips,
I kiss them away.
With your sorrow….
I am carried away…

DESIRE

Naked we come together
Arms intertwine
Lips part and mesh
Kissing you
Desire mounts
Passion's soar.
Descending your body
I define your curves
With tongue lashing fire.
I devour your breasts
In a feast of passion.
Then explore your desire
Intoxicated by your fragrance.
Tasting your offering of love…
Your moist womanhood
Is the unguent
That soothes my parched tongue
As I seek your release
Delving deeper into your loins
My tongue drives your passions
To a roller coaster ride
Of orgasmic delight.

PARADISE'S WELL

The discovery of your body
I will cherish.
The adoration
I lavish upon your body
Will tingle.
My kisses
Will burn like fire.
My caresses
Pulse with electric intensity.
My love
Will sere you
To the core of your emotions,
Taking you higher
With each passing moment,
Until;
You soar upon ecstacie's wings.
Returning you gently
With kisses of love fulfilled,
Resting you in fields of contentment
To caress your heart
With the feathery touch of love.
Gazing upon you
Love flows freely
Returning with the same open intensity
From paradise's well.

HARMONY AND PITCH

Our love an endless melody of emotions
Singing from our hearts
A baritone of desire…
Changing time
The closer we get
A perfect harmony
When we touch.
Together… our love
A symphony
Beating in unison
To the pitch of our being .
Blending out tones
Climbing the scales
To a timbre
We attain as one
Chiming forth
Crystalline beauty
Our souls mate
And sing as one.

AMBROSIA

I want to breathe you
Feel you
Taste you.
I want you
In every corner of my soul.
I want to become your Ambrosia,
To permeate your existence.
I want to feel
The vibrations of your being
And strum the chords of your soul
As we make love.
You are my drug and addiction,
My affliction and cure.
My bittersweet and medicine,
A fountain of youth
Rejuvenating my soul
With our fiery kisses
And searing my loins
With the lava of your love

ONE

One love
One chance
now is the time.
First love
My love for you.
Forever a lifetime.
Two people
You and me,
Once chance
To change two lives.
One heart
Yours to keep.
One dream
The two become one.
One desire
Is all for you
One love
My only love
Never before
Now forever after.

EXPERIENCE II

I want to experience you:
Feel your emotions
Sense your desires
Breathe your passion.
I want to slip into
The fabric of your being.
Meld my mind with yours,
Experience your thoughts and dreams.
I want to become
One with you…
See life
Through your eyes…
Hear the whispering wind
With your ears…
Taste your lust
And savor your love.
I want to experience you.

A FEAST OF YOU

The curve of your hip
The swell of your breasts
The creamy softness of your skin
The sweetness of your lips
The scent of your body
The fragrance of your hair
The power of your love
The taste of your delicacies
A feast filled with desire
A banquet of delight
For a starving Prince

BODY BEAUTIFUL

As I gaze at your picture
My heart races
And I catch my breath in awe
My eyes drink you in
Like the parched earth of a desert landscape
On a rainy day
And trace your curves
As a caress of a moon shadow.
They discern beauty in every detail
As I savor every exposed inch of smooth flesh
And memorize every perfect facet of you.
My eyes only stroke the surface
While my mind consummates your unseen wonders
Revealing every inch of your magnificence.

PERFECTION

Long lustrous hair
Frames the beauty of your face.
Dark waves
That cascade down your back.
A generous halo
Highlighting flawless features.
Stunning eyes
Overflowing with innocence
That shift to sultry
With the promise of love ang passion,
Eyes that smile from a heart
Filled with laughter and a hint of mischief.
Sanguine lips
That speak volumes without a sound.
Soft as rose petals
And even more beautiful
Lips that glow with passion
And beg to be kissed.
The graceful line of your jaw
Defines your ardently beautiful complexion.
Your ultimate grace and beauty
Can only be equated
To one simple word
…perfect…

MUSICAL SORCERESS-HER SECRET

She is beautiful, vibrant and free
A practitioner of an ancient art:
Legendary hero from antiquity
Lifeforce of magic and illusion
Sorceress of unlimited power
Master with an axe in her hands.
The secret of her music…
Her fingers are the instruments
That dance across the strings
Weaving magical sequences
Vibrations that alter time and space.
Images are formed – sounds burst forth
To captivate and dazzle those favored few
With the legacy of her music.

MUSICAL SORCERESS II SIREN'S SONG

A lost and lonely old sea tar
Without charts of bearing…hopeless
Tossed about in life's storms.
A distant voice…her siren song
A melody that captured my heart
Awakening dreams and desires
That lay dormant through the years
Bringing happiness that dried my tears
And rejuvenated my soul
With her power

MUSICAL SORCERESS III
BODY'S SONG

She sings to me with open arms
Inviting me to sample her charms.
Beautiful full red lips
And sensual seductive hips.
Her perky breasts
A perfect place for my head to rest.
Her long legs and sexy butt
They make me dream to see her strut.
The song of her body sings to me
It captivates me then sets me free.

BODY BEAUTIFUL II

The sight of your naked body
Is a breath taking a glorious sun rise.
Your firm breasts and dark nipples
Are as majestic as a high mountain tor.
Your long shapely legs
Are like perfect ivory towers.
Your heart shaped butt
Is as captivating as the harvest moon.
The dark patch of pubic hair
Is my garden of Eden
Leading me into the moist depths
Of the wonderous paradise between your legs
Where I bask in your loving warmth
And frolic with the passions of our love.

SPICE OF LIFE

You are my spice of life
The only flavor
That satisfies my desires.
One taste and I knew
You were the one…
Your fiery love
Is the chili pepper
That scalds my tongue
And sears my loins.
The depth of your emotions
Salt my cheeks and comforting shoulder.
Your care and devotion for me
Are the sweet fragrance of
Honey suckles and cinnamon.
The passion of your kisses
Are wild honey on my lips.
Your gentle caress
Is as soothing as aloe on my skin.
The sweat of your exertions
Is my cool morning dew.
Your radiant smile
Is my dawning of a new day.
The timbre of your laughter
Is the chiming that makes heart sing.
All you are, is what I need
My spice of life
Fulfilling me and sating my appetite.

DEJA VU: TIME PILOT

by
James R. Prince

The year is 3995. Man, in his infinite thirst for knowledge and ultimate arrogance, has altered the human genome, achieving transcendence from the corporeal to the non.

In a state of pure energy, man has cleansed and saved the world he once nearly destroyed.

Not all chose the metamorphosis to a higher non-somatic state of being and were driven off-world––beyond the Sol system––not to be heard from again ... until now.

* * *

Lieutenant Commander Thomas James Fitzpatrick, personal log: I have decided to record a personal log in case anyone ever comes searching. It all began two years ago when General Nin asked me if I'd train to test the new Multi-Atmospheric Aircraft (MAAC). I was put through a battery of tests for health, stress, and things I've never heard of and still can't name. I was then assigned to the NASA training center where I was put through the same rigorous regime as the Shuttle Program. That was the toughest year of my life ... until now.

The training was long and arduous but the bitter resentment the Shuttle crews felt was worst of all. They felt I was an outsider–– stealing into their domain.

The MAAC was built and designed by NASA Aerospace Engineers, thus making me an insurrectionist along for the ride. Finally, the training ended six months ago and the testing began. From day one 'til three days ago there have been nothing but problems. It started with little things, scheduling, so I'm either early or late. Small mechanical problems, the MAAC not pre-flight checked or low on fuel. But until the instrument malfunctions and electrical problems, I hadn't suspected sabotage. It is my opinion certain members of the Shuttle Program were trying their best to insure I would be scrubbed from the MAAC project. The final malfunction came three days ago, July 12th 1995. I'd been looking forward to that day for two years. ——Two years filled with nothing but problems, setbacks, and a few outright failures. But that day would be different. My flight would be a success——I felt it in my bones. So off to work I went with new confidence.

So you understand my arrival in this paradise/pseudo-Earth, I need to explain how the MAAC travels. While flying within the Earth's atmosphere, once the MAAC reaches Mach III the pilot can then use an integral phasing system that allows the MAAC to shift out of phase and accelerate to speeds upwards of sixty thousand miles per hour. On July 12th I was involved in the longest test of the system to date—a twenty-four minute experimental run which would take me completely around the planet. As I re-entered normal phasing something strange happened. I was sent into what I'd call an atypical reverse phasing and experienced a terrible disembodiment before re-entering space-normal in a place devoid of all human life or any sign humans ever inhabited this world.

I've flown from pole to pole and once around the equator. This _is_ the Earth I know, but without any sign of civilization.

Though this may be the Earth I know, I still feel like a stranger. I have no lack of food for this is paradise. The strangest thing is I keep getting the feeling someone or some _thing_ wants me to leave. I've never believed in the supernatural but I'm sure I've heard incomprehensible disembodied voices and felt feathery touches.

I have come to two conclusions. One, I've either entered some form of parallel universe where humans never evolved. Two, I've traveled back in time before man evolved on Earth. I have a third option but as yet I refuse to accept it. Though I feel the touches and hear the voices I know I'm in full control of all my faculties.

This concludes my personal log entry: this, my third day in paradise.

CHAPTER TWO

Lieutenant Commander Thomas James Fitzpatrick, personal log: It is now my twelfth day. I have ceased exploration of my surroundings. I must take flight and see if I can either return to my world or find some form of civilization in this realm. The voices stopped for a couple of days then returned in force——still unintelligible. Now it's to the point I fear for my sanity. My first order of business is to try out-of-phase flight.

Pause log recorder...

* * *

...Continue log entry.

From this point forward my log entry will be in real-time as I try to escape paradise. I'm now strapped in my pilot's chair, all systems check out and I have nominal fuel reserves. Start and lift-off are smooth. Now to accelerate to Mach III.

I'm cruising at fifty thousand feet——all systems operating within acceptable parameters. I'm engaging the phasing drive.

I've now been out of phase for exactly twenty-four minutes, the same amount of time as my test flight. I have re-entered space- normal phasing and my hopes are diminishing as I'm still circling the world I so badly want to leave. I guess my only other option will be to fly into space and send a distress call, hopefully someone will hear. As I increase altitude the stars begin to appear as if they are just over the horizon. This has to be the most awesome sight I've ever seen.

Wow! That was close. As I entered low-Earth-orbit, I almost hit something. I'm lucky to be alive. I just narrowly avoided some form of docking platform. I will go to active sensor search and see what else I should be wary of.

What the sensors are showing is almost beyond belief. According to my on-board computers there are hundreds of space stations and platforms around the planet and the Moon has a heavy concentration of construction on and sub-surface. I believe my best course of action will be to dock at one of the larger stations. I will close this log until I've successfully docked…

…Log continued, day twelve. Docking was unexpectedly easy. Everything is highly automated, as far as I can tell and still in working order. But if everything is still in working order, who is running the station and why wasn't I challenged? The most surprising thing about all this is the fact the docking clamp seemed to be designed for my ship's interface. I am now going to attempt to enter the station. The airlock is standard to the ones I trained on at NASA.

That was as easy as I could have hoped for. I have gained access to the station and from what my environmental suit sensors say, there is breathable air. I am removing my helmet. The air does seem to be fresh and well circulated.

I can see ahead of my present position there appears to be what I think is a computer terminal. I'm going to attempt to access the system and find the Command Center.

It has asked for security codes and none of the ones I know have worked. The strangest thing is I'm still alone. By now I must have caught the attention of someone or set off internal alarms. I will continue my investigation and hope luck pans out in my favor.

A long stretch of surprisingly unproductive log entry punctuated by random grunts and heavy breathing ensued.

* * *

I have now been wandering around these corridors and searching empty rooms for hours and I finally found the Command Center. Everything is shut down so I'll attempt to restore power.

I have restored some of the power systems. Now that I have power to some systems I can hopefully access the files. I haven't done anything but an urgent message has just appeared on one of the monitors. I am stunned by what I am reading.

>From The Council of Beings: The year is 2147. Man has obtained freedom to live outside his physical body. He has evolved to a state of pure energy. Those who refuse to accept this metamorphosis are being forced to leave on ships headed for Alpha Centauri. They believe there is an Earth-like planet to colonize. Those who refuse to leave will be forcibly assimilated into the new order. If you can power up this system, you are still corporeal and warned to leave Sol's system immediately.

End of message.<

I can't believe this! I just spent twelve days on Earth itself and I am now sure I was in the midst of these beings. Though nothing was done to me then, now I've been warned that maybe something will. Worse yet, I have no way to leave Sol's system, much less reach Alpha Centauri. All I can hope to do is figure out how to send a message––assuming it's even possible in time to help me––and pray someone will hear.

CHAPTER THREE

Lieutenant Commander Thomas James Fitzpatrick, personal log, day eighteen: It has been six days since I sent what I believe was a message. I found what is apparently a communications console which employs something called Tachyon Quantum Tunneling. Guess it should work. Hope it works.

I have sent subsequent messages daily, still no response. I am losing hope. I cannot stay on the station much longer. There is plenty of food––resequenced protein––never goes bad, but my water supply is within a couple of days of expiring. I fear I am going to be forced to return to the surface. I am already making my preparations to leave and am stopped by the realization that all the airlocks have recycled and are now under a new code. I must have triggered some stupid internal security protocol. Damn this place!

End personal log, day eighteen...

...Personal log, day, unknown: I have frantically tried everything I know but am effectively trapped forever. I am completely alone with no hope and now no water. The end is near. I've been at the airlock hoping someone or something would release the cycle. My body is so dehydrated my skin has begun to crack and bleed. Several days ago I was reduced to saving moisture by drinking my urine and now that I can no longer urinate, I drink the blood that oozes from my cracked skin. I have no strength to continue this personal log. Though I doubt anyone will ever read or hear this it is here for anyone to find.

What?

I hear something, some kind of alarm or beeping tone. I'm fading to the gray area between life and death but the beeping continues and is getting louder. I close my eyes.

I open my eyes in bed as some strange dream slowly fades. Time to go to work. Today is the final test flight of the MAAC. I've been looking forward to this day for two years. Two years filled with nothing but problems, setbacks, and a few outright failures. But today will be different. My flight will be a success——I feel it in my bones.

THE END